USBORNE
COLOUR YOUR OWN
SUPERHEROES

Designed by Marc Maynard and Claire Thomas
Written by Sam Smith

Illustrated by Gong Studios

FUZE

Fuze's skin ripples, then suddenly splits apart so an incoming attack hits only empty air. Made up of billions of microbots flying in formation, this shape-shifter can infiltrate anywhere to give the heroes the upper hand

COAX

"SLEEEEEEEP, AND HEAR MY WORDS," Coax croons as she sprinkle[s] dust into people's ears. A tiny, brilliant tactician, she rides silent[ly] on the wind, turning adversaries into allies to bring about peac[e].

DATA

- **SKILL:** 7
- **SPEED:** 6
- **STRENGTH:** 1
- **INTELLECT:** 9
- **POWER:** flight, mind control, very hard to detect

CYBERDRON

DATA

- SKILL: 7
- SPEED: 7
- STRENGTH: 3
- INTELLECT: 10
- POWER: genius-level intellect, computer expert

This digital mastermind surfs the clouds, deploying drones to boost his brainwaves. Hacking into criminals' systems, he soon turns their own technology against them.

SAND DRAGON

DATA
- SKILL: 4
- SPEED: 7
- STRENGTH: 9
- INTELLECT: 3
- POWER: super strength, breathes sleeping gas

When a threat looms, Sergeant Drake leaps into action and becomes Sand Dragon. Four-armed and fierce, he overpowers villains, then subdues them with his sleep breath.

KOLOSSAL

"YOU DARE ATTACK ME?!" Kolossal booms. Exiled from the giant planet Vast, he swats alien ships like flies and flings them back into space to defend Earth – his new home.

DATA

- **SKILL:** 4
- **SPEED:** 5
- **STRENGTH:** 10
- **INTELLECT:** 6
- **POWER:** super strength and toughness, advanced weaponry

SPHERE

DATA

- **SKILL:** ■■■■■■■ 7
- **SPEED:** 7
- **STRENGTH:** ■■■■ 5
- **INTELLECT:** 7
- **POWER:** creates impenetrable shield around herself

At the heart of the battle, Sphere deploys her impenetrable shield, and plasma-blasts fizzle like wet fireworks as she hurries to help her friends.

VULKANO

DATA

- **SKILL:** ▮▮▮▮▮▮▮ 7
- **SPEED:** ▯▯▯▯ 4
- **STRENGTH:** ▮▮▮▮▮▮▮ 7
- **INTELLECT:** ▯▯▯▯▯▯ 6
- **POWER:** shoots flame from either hand, fire-resistant

Veins of scorching magma flow beneath Vulkano's rocky exterior. Suddenly, his molten core glows deep crimson, lava erupts from his fists and he hurls a red-hot fireball at his foe.

HACKER

DATA

• SKILL:	■■■■■■■	8
• SPEED:		7
• STRENGTH:	■■	3
• INTELLECT:		9

• **POWER:** computer master, almost infinite knowledge

An advanced AI experiment, this digital mischief-maker walks through enemy firewalls for fun. Cloning identities in an instant, he taps into limitless data to keep the heroes ten steps ahead.

ERAZER

When defeat looms, Erazer can still turn the tide. Slicing through time with her crescent-moon charm, she races into the rift to alter history.

DATA

- **SKILL:** 9
- **SPEED:** 8
- **STRENGTH:** 4
- **INTELLECT:** 7
- **POWER:** time travel between past and present

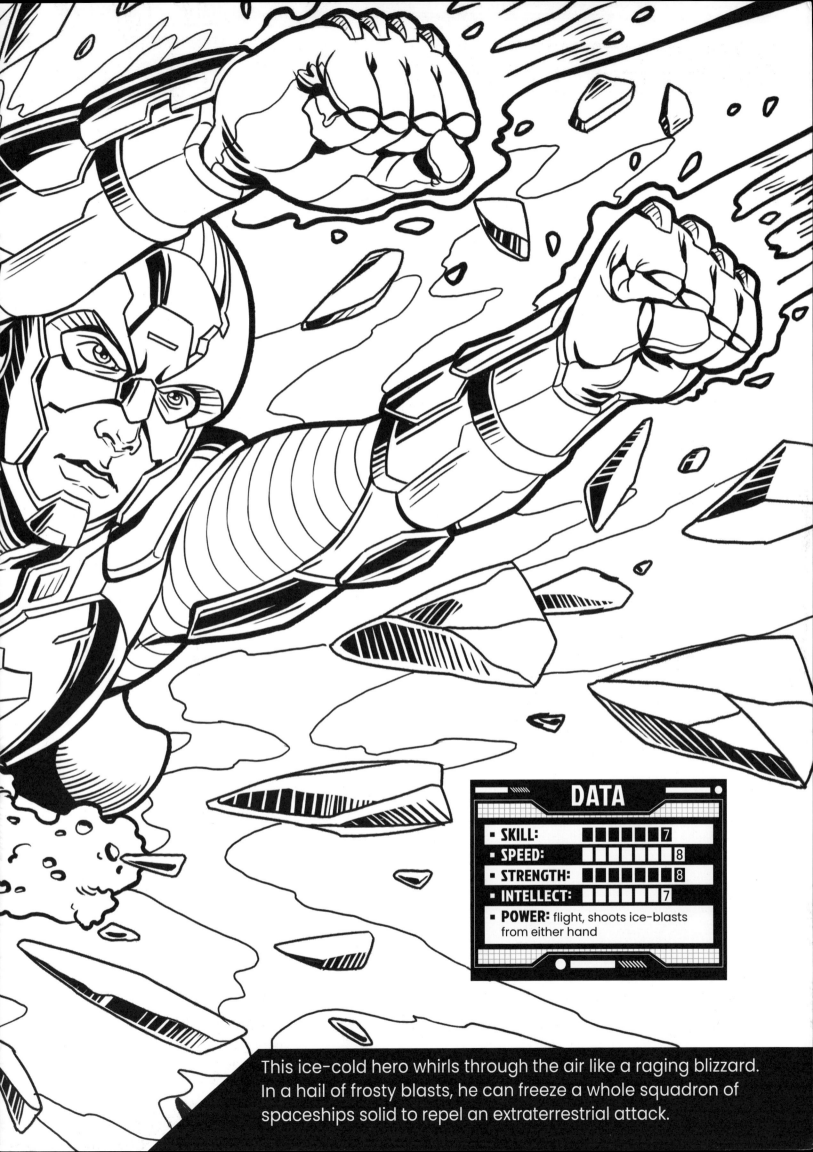

DATA

- **SKILL:** ▮▮▮▮▮▮▮ 7
- **SPEED:** ▮▮▮▮▮▮▮▮ 8
- **STRENGTH:** ▮▮▮▮▮▮▮▮ 8
- **INTELLECT:** ▮▮▮▮▮▮▮ 7
- **POWER:** flight, shoots ice-blasts from either hand

This ice-cold hero whirls through the air like a raging blizzard. In a hail of frosty blasts, he can freeze a whole squadron of spaceships solid to repel an extraterrestrial attack.

KRUNCH

DATA

- **SKILL:** 4
- **SPEED:** 4
- **STRENGTH:**
- **INTELLECT:** 2
- **POWER:** super strength and toughness, feels no pain

Possessing enough power to forge mountains and carve out coastlines, this ancient Earth guardian has protected the planet for millions of years.

GRIP

DATA

- **SKILL:** ▪▪▪▪▪▪▪▪▪▪ 10
- **SPEED:** ▪▪▪▪▪▪▪ 7
- **STRENGTH:** ▪▪ 3
- **INTELLECT:** ▪▪▪▪▪▪ 6
- **POWER:** can climb anything, telescopic vision, sharpshooter

Grip scurries up walls with reptilian stealth, silent and unseen. Her forked tongue tastes the air, then – SHOONK! – a magic arrow sends the target to sleep.

DRAKONA

Mai Ito vanished years ago near a mysterious mountain temple. Reborn as the ninja Drakona, she moves like a ghost, vanquishing villains with a swish of her robes.

DATA

- **SKILL:** 10
- **SPEED:** 8
- **STRENGTH:** 5
- **INTELLECT:** 5
- **POWER:** expert martial artist, super agility and reflexes

HURACAN

Huracan's medallion crackles with ancient power. Suddenly, lightning forks flash from his eyes and the wind howls as he summons up the ultimate storm.

VOIDE

DATA

- **SKILL:** `■■■■■■■■■` 9
- **SPEED:** `■■■■■■■` 7
- **STRENGTH:** `■■■■■■` 6
- **INTELLECT:** `■■■■■■■` 7
- **POWER:** wields dark-energy rift lance, controls space dragon

Riding a space dragon, Voide covers light years in a single leap. With a slash of her rift lance, she locks intergalactic outlaws deep inside another dimension.

XPONENTIAL

DATA

- **SKILL:** 6
- **SPEED:** 4
- **STRENGTH:** 6
- **INTELLECT:** 8
- **POWER:** self-replication, can be everywhere at once

Xponential clones himself at will to isolate any threat. Multiplying at dizzying speed, he bamboozles enemies and single-handedly defuses the danger.

CHASM

DATA

- **SKILL:** `▮▮▮▮▮▮▮▮` 8
- **SPEED:** `▮▮▮▮▮` 5
- **STRENGTH:** `▮▮▮▮▮▮▮▮▮` 9
- **INTELLECT:** `▮▮▮▮▮` 5
- **POWER:** controls tides, waves and whirlpools, possibly immortal

An unknown entity from the depths, Chas manipulates the tides. Soothing the ocea with strange words, she turns tsunamis harmlessly aside to keep cities safe.

COLONEL LASER

This bionic supersoldier is a one-man battalion. His powerful laser cannons will pierce any shield, taking down multiple targets in a split second.

DATA

- SKILL: ▮▮▮▮▮▮▮▮ 8
- SPEED: ▯▯▯▯ 4
- STRENGTH: ▮▮▮▮▮▮ 6
- INTELLECT: ▮▮▮▮▮▮ 6
- POWER: suit targets multiple enemies, sees through walls

HORUS SA

DATA

- **SKILL:** ▮▮▮▮▮▮▮▮ 8
- **SPEED:** ▮▮▮▮ 4
- **STRENGTH:** ▮▮▮▮▮ 5
- **INTELLECT:** ▮▮▮▮▮▮▮▮ 8
- **POWER:** summons sand army, mace shoots heat rays

Wielding the mace of the sun, Horus Sa cries "WARRIORS… AWAKE!" and summons his sand army. When aliens attacked in 2064, he swept over Earth's enemies like a desert tide, and buried their starships deep under the dunes.

MASON

Mason's orbs swirl around her like basilisk eyes, then – ZAP! Striking forward at blinding speed, a ball of supercharged plasma sends the villain crashing back as a block of stone.

DATA

- **SKILL:** 10
- **SPEED:** 9
- **STRENGTH:** 4
- **INTELLECT:** 6
- **POWER:** turns opponents to stone, lightning-fast reflexes

LEONA

DATA

▪ **SKILL:**	■■■■■■■□	8
▪ **SPEED:**	■■■■■■■□	8
▪ **STRENGTH:**	■■■■■■■□	8
▪ **INTELLECT:**	■■■■■	5

▪ **POWER:** super agility and reflexes, deafening roar

Unsheathing claws that can punch holes in steel, Leona climbs with cat-like grace. Her thundering roar stuns the enemy, then she pounces on her prey.